DATE DUE

Demco No. 62-0549

Leaving Vietnam

The Journey of Tuan Ngo, a Boat Boy

by Sarah S. Kilborne
illustrated by Melissa Sweet

READY-TO-READ
ALADDIN PAPERBACKS

First Aladdin Paperbacks Edition, February 1999

Text copyright © 1999 by Sarah S. Kilborne
Illustrations copyright © 1999 by Melissa Sweet

Aladdin Paperbacks
An imprint of Simon & Schuster Children's Publishing Division
1230 Avenue of the Americas
New York, NY 10020

READY-TO-READ is a registered trademark
of Simon & Schuster, Inc.

Also available in a Simon & Schuster Books for Young Readers edition.

The text of this book was set in Utopia.
Printed and bound in the United States of America

10 9 8 7 6 5 4 3 2 1

The Library of Congress has cataloged the hardcover edition
as follows:
Kilborne, Sarah S.
Leaving Vietnam : the journey of Tuan Ngo, a boat boy / by Sarah S.
Kilborne ; illustrated by Melissa Sweet.
p. cm. — (Ready-to-read)
Summary: Tells the story of a boy and his father who endure danger
and difficulties when they escape by boat from Vietnam,
spend days at sea, and then months in refugee camps
before making their way to the United States.
ISBN 0-689-80798-8(hc)
1. Vietnam—History—1975- —Juvenile literature. 2. Refugees,
Political—Vietnam—Juvenile literature. 3. Ngo, Tuan. [1. Ngo, Tuan.
2. Refugees—Vietnam.] I. Sweet, Melissa, ill. II. Title. III. Series
Ds559.912.K55 1998
959.704'4—dc21
97-15061
CIP
AC
ISBN 0-689-80797-X (pbk.)

Contents

1. The Escape 5

2. At Sea 15

3. The Pirates 20

4. We Are Rescued 23

5. The Small, Windy Island 28

6. The Final Camps 34

7. America at Last! 43

HANOI

LAOS

THAILAND

CAMBODIA

VIETNAM

BIEN HOA
(TUAN NGO'S HOME)

HO CHI MINH

4

CHAPTER ONE
The Escape

"Let's go, Tuan Ngo," my father says. I put on a black shirt and black pants. I fill my pockets with grandmother's gold and take off my shoes. We leave. It is the middle of the night.

We bend down like cranes and go fast into the woods. We meet other people in a circle of trees. They wear black too but I don't know any of them. Then my uncle appears. He stands on his toes and counts our heads with a stick.

"Thirty-three," he says.

"That is too many," my father whispers.

I watch a boy who is younger than I am. He hides behind his father. My uncle waves his arms. He points to where the boat will be, someplace far away, and we follow him through the trees.

No one says a word. If we're caught, we'll be put in a labor camp for five years. My father was in a labor camp for six years, and he says that all he ate there were

rotten potatoes. I don't want to eat rotten potatoes. So I watch my feet and where I step. I pretend I have eyes like an owl. It is so dark. There is no moon.

We walk for a long, long time, through forests and mud and water. Sometimes I step on a thorn or a piece of old iron and

my feet bleed because I have no shoes. But I don't cry or ask for help. I just keep going like everyone else.

When I see the boat, I am scared. Everyone else is scared too. We stand on the beach and look. It is a fishing boat and it is not far from shore. But it is tiny. My father was right. There are too many of us. The cabin in the middle is so small it looks like a peanut.

Two teenage boys start to shake. Their mouths open wide and I think they are going to scream but they don't. They twist around and run back into the trees like wild wolves. I want to go with them, back to my mother and brothers at home.

"At least now there is room on the boat," my father says. And he reminds me that we are going to America and we are going to help save the rest of our family from the

9

Viet Cong soldiers. We will make lots of money in America. Then we will send it to my mother. She will hide it in the fields. When she has two thousand dollars, she and my younger brothers will be able to escape too.

My uncle pushes a rowboat onto the beach. This rowboat was hidden in some trees and will take us to our boat. I help load it with rice and water and a drink made from lemons and sugar. Then I climb in.

I sit very still between my father and a woman with big feet. She presses her heels together again and again. The rowboat wobbles. I touch my pockets to make sure

my grandmother's jewelry is still there—two gold necklaces. We'll need the gold to trade for money.

When we get to our boat we sit down wherever we can. My father and I each take a corner but now we are far apart from each other. I want to change places, but my uncle turns on the motor. The boat

jumps forward. Then *whoosh!* The right
side dips into the water. People tumble.
"The anchor! Lift up the anchor!" someone
shouts. I hold onto the left side, now high
in the air, and I scream. Everybody
screams. We can't help it. But my uncle is
fast and he grabs the anchor and then
guns the engine to speed us away.

The harbor guards have heard us and they come after us, firing and shouting, "Stop!" We keep going. I duck my head and close my eyes. Gunshots. I cover up my ears and try not to listen. But soon all I hear is the motor. We have escaped. We are on our way.

CHAPTER TWO
At Sea

For five days and nights we move along the sea. I crawl to my father's side and lean against him. I smell his hair and his clothes and watch the water. We don't have to be quiet anymore, but no one says anything. We are tired and thirsty and sick. There is throw-up all over.

Some people say they're going to jump overboard. But my uncle tells them that sharks will eat them and the salt water will burn their skin. They cry and cry and other people begin to shout at them and everyone goes crazy.

An old man starts to scream, "The Viet

Cong are coming!" over and over again. He thinks the enemy is after him, right here in the boat. He yells across to me, "They're going to kill us!"

The old man wants to go back to Vietnam and die in the country where he was born. He dives into the water where all the sharks are and tries to swim away. The biggest men go in after him and pull him back. He tries to bite them. They tie him up with a rope, around and around, and put him in the cabin. I look at my father. He is praying.

On the third day the engine breaks down. It spits like a baby. Then it stops, and we drift. And drift. My uncle can do nothing. He leans against a woman who leans against another woman who leans against the cabin. They stare at the water.

Two big fish swim by us. They are as big as our boat but they are not sharks. We see their fins and sometimes their tails. They don't hurt us. I like that.

On the fourth day we are out of food and water. My stomach hurts, but I tell myself it doesn't. I wonder what my mother is doing at home. I miss her so much. She is probably selling rice in the marketplace like she always does. And my brothers are probably inside playing. I want to be inside too. The sun will not go away. It burns me and makes me so thirsty. All I wish for is a little bit of rain, just a drop

in my mouth. Then I see a great thing.

"Look, Papa!" I shout.

There is a cloud and rain coming towards us. Soon I am soaking wet. I stand with my mouth open and try to drink as much of the rain as I can. I shake my hair and wipe the salt off my skin. My father claps his hands, and we laugh and laugh. It is raining!

CHAPTER THREE
The Pirates

That afternoon we see three boats that are bigger than ours. We jump up and down and wave and shout, "Over here! Help! Over here!" We make a flag out of a towel and my uncle waves it above his head.

The three boats circle us. When they come really close we can see the men have dark curly hair and dark skin and all they wear is black underwear. They look wild. They yell, "Kneel down!" They point guns at us. They are pirates!

One of the boats comes right next to ours. Its captain throws down a rope and orders us to take it and climb onto his ship.

We're so afraid that we forget about the

old crazy man in the cabin. We climb up the rope and leave him there. Suddenly we hear him yelling, "Viet Cong! Viet Cong!" and right after that we hear a *splash!* He's jumped overboard but he's still all tied up! Some of the pirates dive into the water and bring him back to the ship. They put him down at our feet. He drips and shakes and I try to get away from him. I don't want the pirates to think I like him.

The pirates search our boat and our clothes and they take our gold jewelry. But they feel sorry for us. They give us water and fix up our boat and put fuel in the engine. They even give us directions to land. My father whispers, "It's a miracle!" and hugs me close.

We climb the rope back down to our boat. I look over the side at the pirates. We move away. The pirate boats stay where they are.

CHAPTER FOUR
We Are Rescued

We see another ship the next day, but the sun is high and beating off its sides, and all I see everywhere is light. When the ship comes closer, I can tell it's made of iron and steel. It is the largest boat I have ever seen. My uncle says it's a German ship carrying oil.

We shout at the men on deck but they don't want to help us. We are losing strength. We beg, "Please! Please!" They still don't help. Some of them walk away, back inside their big boat.

"They cannot leave us here," my father says. "They have to help us!"

Everyone agrees. Then we do something

scary. We break our boat. A man puts a hole in the bottom so the Germans will think that we're sinking. And we *are* sinking!

Our plan works. The Germans drop us a rope ladder. But I can't move. My legs feel tingly and they won't stand up. A man with big arms climbs down and lifts me to his shoulder. I look into his white face. He smiles at me.

When we are all on the German ship, we look back at our tiny boat. We watch it disappear under the water. I see bubbles and foam. I am not sad. My heart is like a

stone. I am glad that boat is gone and I will never have to sit in it again.

One of our men speaks English. He talks with the Germans, who speak English too. Then they give us apples and grapes and soda and lots of good food. We have a feast!

At home we had so little food because of the Viet Cong. They wanted everything for themselves. My family was lucky because my mom sold rice. She hid rice for us that was supposed to be given to the Viet Cong. All we ate every day was rice, potatoes, and corn mixed together.

The Germans say we can spend the night wherever we find room. My father and I find an empty stairway. The stairs are bumpy and cold but we aren't outside anymore, and the water's not spraying me. It is like heaven here.

We stay many days. Then we have to go. The captain says they don't have enough food to keep feeding us. They will drop us off at a nearby island. The island has a refugee camp for Vietnamese people like us, who have escaped by boat and want to go to America.

CHAPTER FIVE

The Small, Windy Island

It is nice to be on land. And this island has electricity and mail. We get to send a letter to my mother. We tell her we are alright. We have survived the South China Sea.

But the island is not American, and I don't want to stay here. The camp is crowded and new. The men in charge don't have food for all the people. They give us uncooked rice and when we are lucky we get meat in a can.

My father and I stay close to our friends from the boat. We help each other. At night it is very cold. We have no clothes except for the shirts and shorts we are wearing, so we huddle and keep each other warm. We give each other chores. Some people make the fire we cook on. Others make bowls from coconut shells. Some hunt for twigs to use as chopsticks. My father and I pick fruit from the trees and search for plants we can eat.

The building we sleep in is a barrack. Its walls are green plastic sheets. Sometimes the sheets blow off in the wind. It is scary to close my eyes. And it

is painful to sleep. Our beds are hard wood planks. One lantern hangs from the ceiling.

My father and I are interviewed on this island. So is everyone else from our boat. The men in charge ask us our names and the day we were born and where we come from in Vietnam. Then the men go back to their offices and find out if what we say is true. They tell us this will take many weeks. My father and I pray every day that none of our friends is a liar. If anyone lies, the whole boat will be sent back to Vietnam. And the Viet Cong soldiers will be mean to us since we tried to get away from them.

Each day more refugees come to the island. I stand on the beach and watch them arrive. I don't play with other children or grown-ups. Many people are yellow. They have malaria and are dying

31

and I have to be careful not to get sick like them. My mother and brothers need me. My father says that he needs me too. There are hills behind our barrack. I want to know what's on the other side of them, but pirates could be there so I don't go exploring.

Two moons pass. The report from our interviews comes back. I am so nervous, but then my father tells me everybody said the truth! We can leave this place. My father says now we are going to someplace else that is closer to America.

CHAPTER SIX
The Final Camps

A big round boat with no windows takes us to another island. This island is much bigger than the last one. There are more hills. There is more sand. And it is dry and hot, but I think it is better. The men in charge give us spoons and bowls and towels and soap. They even give us clothes! And they tell us we'll get rice and fish *every day*. I see cars and schools and a marketplace, too.

I look around for the yellow people who are dying but there aren't any. Instead, I see one of my older cousins. He is standing in front of a barrack.

"Tuyen!" I shout. I grab my father's arm.

"Look who it is! Look who it is!"

Tuyen left Vietnam two years ago. My family didn't know if he was still alive. My father is so happy. The two of them talk for a long time while we stand on the street. Tuyen tells my father what life is like here. He says it is very boring. There is a lot of waiting. And we will be interviewed many times more.

There are two camps on this island. We are in the first. Here we will be told if we can really say good-bye to Vietnam and the Viet Cong soldiers. If that is so, then we go to the second camp. In the second camp we choose another country to live in.

Some people in the first camp are spies. Some people lie. Everybody has to be checked again and again. The wait in Camp One can be many, many years.

A week later in the marketplace, Tuyen's name is called from a list. He gets to go to the second camp! I think that is incredible for him.

"See you in America!" my father and I say, and we wave. A car takes Tuyen away. Then we are alone again with just our friends from the boat.

I go to the marketplace a lot after that. Every month a man with big teeth stands at one end and reads the important list. I get right in front of him and watch his mouth. He does not want to say my

father's name. I start to not trust this man. He does not help us.

Each Saturday I clean up some of the camp. All the men have to do this. My other days I am free. I don't go to school because I feel so shy. I look at the candies in the marketplace. I play marbles with some boys.

At home we used to climb mango trees and there wasn't red dust all over. But here there is more peace. Men with guns don't stand around everywhere. People don't get hurt.

Five months in a row the man with big teeth does not call my father's name. But the sixth time he does.

"Papa!" I yell. "Papa, we can go to the second camp!"

My father and I cannot stop smiling. We say good-bye to our friends and my uncle from the boat. It is sad for them but good for us. We wish everyone much luck.

The second camp looks like the first. But it is American and the best place yet. My father and I are given an apartment! We have a stove and more food than two people can eat. My father and I send a letter to my mother. We think we are going to make it! We send a letter to my mother's uncle in America to see if he will let us come live with him. He escaped from Vietnam three years before we left. He writes back, "Yes!" And he says Cousin Tuyen is there with him!

But the Americans have to make sure that everything is okay. We will have to wait some more. This is hard to do. But we make new friends. I play marbles with other boys. My father and I go to the movies. Every week they show a Kung Fu movie for free on an outdoor screen.

One month goes by. Two months go by. Three months go by. Four months go by. I start to grow again. I didn't realize I had stopped. But now I eat more food so I begin to get taller. Five months go by. My

father does not lose hope. He says to me, "We'll be alright." Six months go by. But six must be a special number.

My father's name is read from the last important list!

Then everything happens so fast. We pack our clothes and our bowls and spoons. We get on a boat. It takes us to Singapore. A car drives us to the airport. And there is the plane.

CHAPTER SEVEN
America at Last!

The plane is huge and loud. But I know it is safe and this plane goes to America, so it must be good. I sit in an orange seat and watch my father. He is scared too, and he closes his eyes. The engines roar. They speed us forward and suddenly we're in the air. My heart jumps. I watch Singapore's buildings get smaller and smaller until they look like grains of rice. Then I see the clouds. They're right outside the window!

We land in San Francisco, California, the United States of America. I saw pictures of America back in Vietnam. My father showed me magazines with tall people and big

cars. My grandparents told me America was a country of gold where people were happy. And now I am here.

My father picks me up and hugs me tight and begins to cry. I cry too but keep my eyes open so I won't miss anything. Everyone is so white. I look at my arms. I am so dark. I have been living on islands for a year. My father is really dark, too.

I can't believe we have come so far. I

can't believe we are alive. And tomorrow we will be in Philadelphia with my uncle and Cousin Tuyen. We will live with them and I will go to school. My father will work and we'll be able to send for my mother and brothers.

But tonight we stay in a hotel. The beds are soft and cool and their sheets are folded back into triangles. I pick up a machine by my bed.

"What is this?" I ask my father.

"Don't touch that!" he says. "It's a telephone!"

A telephone! My family didn't have one in Vietnam. But I have heard about them. And my father says he has used one before.

"Papa," I ask, "will you show me?" I'll be just like an American boy and talk to my uncle and cousin far away in their home.

"Yes," he says. "But it is the middle of the night, Tuan Ngo. And it's time to go to sleep."

I dream that my family and all of my friends are free.

AFTERWORD

After World War II, Vietnam, a small country in Southeast Asia, suffered a long, bitter civil war. The North Vietnamese, or Viet Cong, won this war in 1975 and then began persecuting their enemy, the South Vietnamese, whom the French and the Americans had supported. Tuan Ngo's family was from South Vietnam, and Tuan's dad had been a soldier in the South Vietnamese army. When the war ended, they, like many others, feared for their safety and their future.

Refugees like Tuan and his dad were called "boat people" because they usually fled by fishing boat on the South China Sea. Many boats sank and hopeful people died, but they were willing to take the risk rather than live under Viet Cong rule.

In 1983, when Tuan was eleven years old, he and his dad arrived safely in the United States. Three years later, Tuan's mother and brothers made it to the States as well, and the family was reunited.

They do not know what happened to everyone else. Some people on Tuan Ngo's boat followed Tuan and his dad to Philadelphia. Others went to Canada or Australia. A few, unfortunately, had to stay behind in the camps. For two years, Tuan and his dad received letters from these people, but then, for reasons unknown, the letters stopped.

Tuan still lives with family and friends in Philadelphia. His parents have even had four more children! Someday, Tuan hopes to go back to Vietnam. But now, America is his home.

5881